Hanukkah Moon

By Deborah da Costa

Illustrated by Gosia Mosz

KAR-BEN
PUBLISHING

For cousin Elliott who long ago introduced me to the bird tree,
and for my darlings Harry and Owen, who will one day get to read about it.

With special thanks to Elizabeth and Victor Coronado for the
Mexican Hanukkah song, to Margaret Cohen and Cynthia Wassong
for their amazing computer skills, and to Anthony, Danit, Gene, Warren,
and the Sunday Group for their continuing support.
— D. D.

Dedicated to my dearest Andrzej.
— G. M.

AUTHOR'S NOTE

Hanukkah celebrates a time more than 2,000 years ago, when a small group of Jews fought the army of Syria and took back the holy city of Jerusalem. Then the Jews rebuilt their ruined Temple and lit the Temple's sacred lamp. Legend has it that despite very little oil, the lamp miraculously burned for eight days and eight nights. Hanukkah celebrates a time when the few defeated the many and religious freedom was restored. Today, Jewish families celebrate by lighting the Hanukkah menorah (hanukkiah), eating traditional foods, and exchanging gifts. Jewish communities and families around the world have their own special customs.

This story reflects the celebration of the new moon that occurs during Hanukkah. This custom is popular among Sephardic Jews (those whose ancestors came from Spain), who settled in Latin America.

It is dark the morning we leave for Aunt Luisa's house. I breathe foggy clouds into the air.

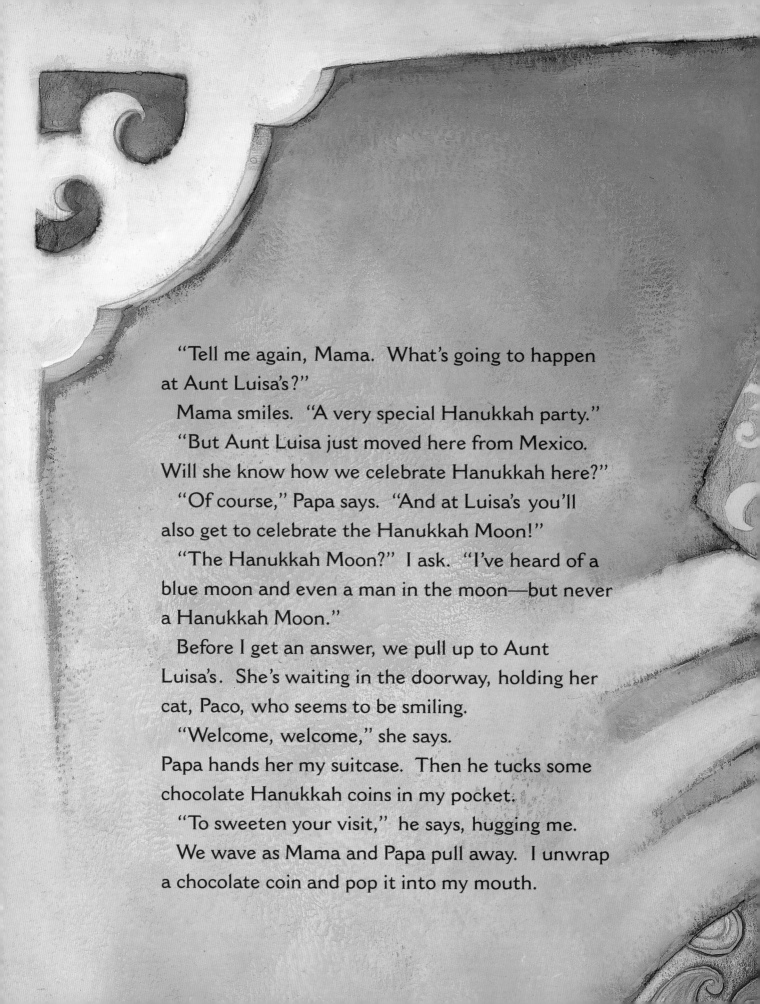

"Tell me again, Mama. What's going to happen at Aunt Luisa's?"

Mama smiles. "A very special Hanukkah party."

"But Aunt Luisa just moved here from Mexico. Will she know how we celebrate Hanukkah here?"

"Of course," Papa says. "And at Luisa's you'll also get to celebrate the Hanukkah Moon!"

"The Hanukkah Moon?" I ask. "I've heard of a blue moon and even a man in the moon—but never a Hanukkah Moon."

Before I get an answer, we pull up to Aunt Luisa's. She's waiting in the doorway, holding her cat, Paco, who seems to be smiling.

"Welcome, welcome," she says. Papa hands her my suitcase. Then he tucks some chocolate Hanukkah coins in my pocket.

"To sweeten your visit," he says, hugging me.

We wave as Mama and Papa pull away. I unwrap a chocolate coin and pop it into my mouth.

Aunt Luisa's house is filled with colorful rugs and lots of photos on the walls. I admire a shiny pink banner over the fireplace which says FELIZ JANUCA! The letters are made out of tiny photos of birds.

"That means 'Happy Hanukkah' in Spanish," Aunt
Luisa explains. "The birds are from my bird tree." She
points toward a huge, bare-branched tree in her backyard.

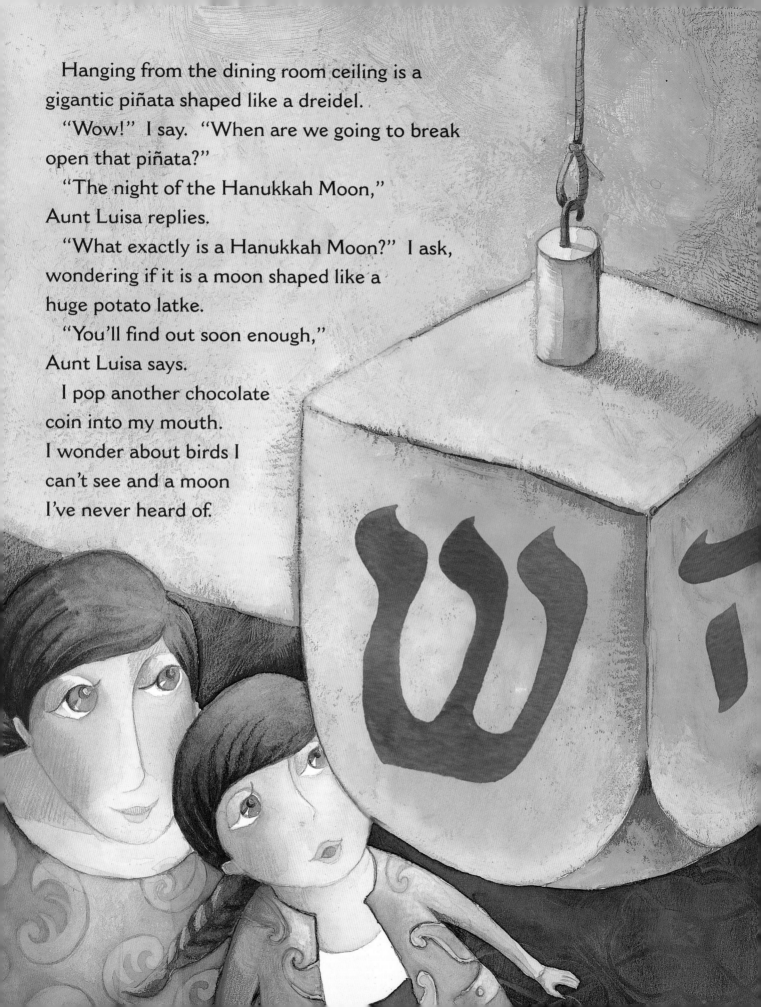

Hanging from the dining room ceiling is a
gigantic piñata shaped like a dreidel.

"Wow!" I say. "When are we going to break
open that piñata?"

"The night of the Hanukkah Moon,"
Aunt Luisa replies.

"What exactly is a Hanukkah Moon?" I ask,
wondering if it is a moon shaped like a
huge potato latke.

"You'll find out soon enough,"
Aunt Luisa says.

I pop another chocolate
coin into my mouth.
I wonder about birds I
can't see and a moon
I've never heard of.

In the kitchen window is a big hanukkiah that looks
like a boat with birds, squirrels, raccoons,
and deer.

"I like your hanukkiah," I tell Aunt Luisa. "I've
never seen one like it."

"I made it myself," she says. "It's my little Noah's
Ark. I modeled it after my backyard friends."

I look out the window. The backyard is empty.
I guess Aunt Luisa has a great imagination.

That night we celebrate by lighting the hanukkiah and eating latkes. I give Aunt Luisa a little silver dreidel from Israel. She gives me a small package wrapped in shiny blue paper. It's a little camera.

I take pictures of Paco sleeping on his back, Paco playing with a ball, and Paco looking out the window.

Aunt Luisa smiles. "I'm glad you like taking pictures, Isobel. Maybe you can visit one of my photography classes."

"You take classes?" I ask.

"I teach them," she answers, "at the university. You'll get to meet some of my students soon."

I look outside again before I go to bed. There is
hardly any moon—just a tiny sliver of light. I fall
asleep dreaming of a moon shaped like a giant
dreidel that pops open showering the world with
Hanukkah gifts.

Aunt Luisa wakes me early. The sun is just coming up. "Quick," she says. "Throw on your coat and slippers. And take your camera."

We walk toward the bird tree. "Shhh," she says. "Walk softly."

The tree is full of birds chirping and buzzing and pecking away at feeders.

"Take some pictures," she whispers. "Then we can look in my bird book and see which ones they are."

I take lots and lots of pictures. Aunt Luisa
takes some, too. When we are finished, we go
back to the house for jelly doughnuts and cocoa.
While Aunt Luisa prints the pictures, I get
dressed. When I look outside again, the sun is
up, but the birds are gone.

Aunt Luisa spreads our photos out on the dining room table next to her bird book. We have taken pictures of black-capped chickadees, cardinals, kinglets, and blue jays. The chickadees are wearing little black hats that look like yarmulkes. Maybe they are Hanukkah birds and maybe they will bring the Hanukkah Moon.

That night after we light the hanukkiah, Aunt Luisa
gives me a beautiful scrapbook of our bird photos.
Outside, the moon has gotten even smaller.

I wake up to a delicious smell. Aunt Luisa is baking dreidel-shaped cookies.

As I help her cut them out, I sing: "Dreidel, dreidel, dreidel. I made it out of clay."

Aunt Luisa sings back, "Trompo, trompo, trompo, lo hice de barro."

We sing more verses in English and Spanish while we
sprinkle the cookies with colored sugar. I eat two before
Aunt Luisa stops me. "You can have plenty more tonight
when we celebrate the Hanukkah Moon."

At last! I will get to see the mysterious Hanukkah Moon.
I help Aunt Luisa cut vegetables for couscous. We brush
Paco until his fur shines.

Aunt Luisa puts plates of grapes, nuts,
and berries outside on a low table. She
adds a small bowl of water.

"We may have some surprise visitors
tonight," she tells me.

"Why don't we just invite them in?"
I ask.

Aunt Luisa just laughs, and I wonder if
these surprise guests have bad manners.

It's starting to get dark when Aunt Luisa's students arrive.
They kiss Aunt Luisa on the cheek and shake my hand.
"Isobel, meet Vida, Batsheva, and Naomi," Aunt Luisa says.
Vida is carrying a huge bunch of flowers, Batsheva holds a
straw basket filled with little boxes of sweets, and Naomi has
two cameras dangling from her shoulders.

We join Aunt Luisa in blessing the lights. She adds a special reading. "Tonight is Rosh Hodesh, the beginning of a new month and an important time for women. You remember that when Moses came down from Mt. Sinai with the Ten Commandments, he found the Israelites worshipping a golden calf. According to tradition, the women refused to contribute their gold to help build the idol. Their reward was a special holiday once a month—Rosh Hodesh—the time of the new moon."

"Wow!" I say. "I didn't know that!"

After dinner, it's time to break open the piñata.
I stand on a chair and whack it hard with a stick
while Aunt Luisa holds me tight.   Out fall bags of
chocolate coins and tiny prizes.
   "Wow and double wow!" is all I can say.
"This is the best Hanukkah!"
   "It's not over yet," Aunt Luisa says.
"Let's go outside."

It's very dark on Aunt Luisa's porch. The sky is black as ink. And there is no moon at all! It has disappeared like the morning birds.

"Shhh," Aunt Luisa whispers. "We don't want to scare away our guests."

"But where is the Hanukkah Moon?" I whisper.

Aunt Luisa points toward the sky. "It's there," she says. "It is the luna nueva, the new moon that always appears during Hanukkah."

"But why can't I see it?" I ask.

"Because the bright side is facing away from the earth," she explains. "Tomorrow night it will start to reappear."

My eyes are getting used to the dark. And now I can see the guests. Two deer and a fat raccoon are eating the nuts and berries Aunt Luisa left for them.

"Look," I whisper.

"Yes," she whispers back. "They come in the dark when they feel safe."

While we watch, Aunt Luisa's students take pictures with their special night cameras. When all the food is gone, the animals disappear and we go inside.

As the guests leave, we wish each other a Hodesh Tov, a good month.

That night I dream about a moon, birds, and animals that appear and disappear.

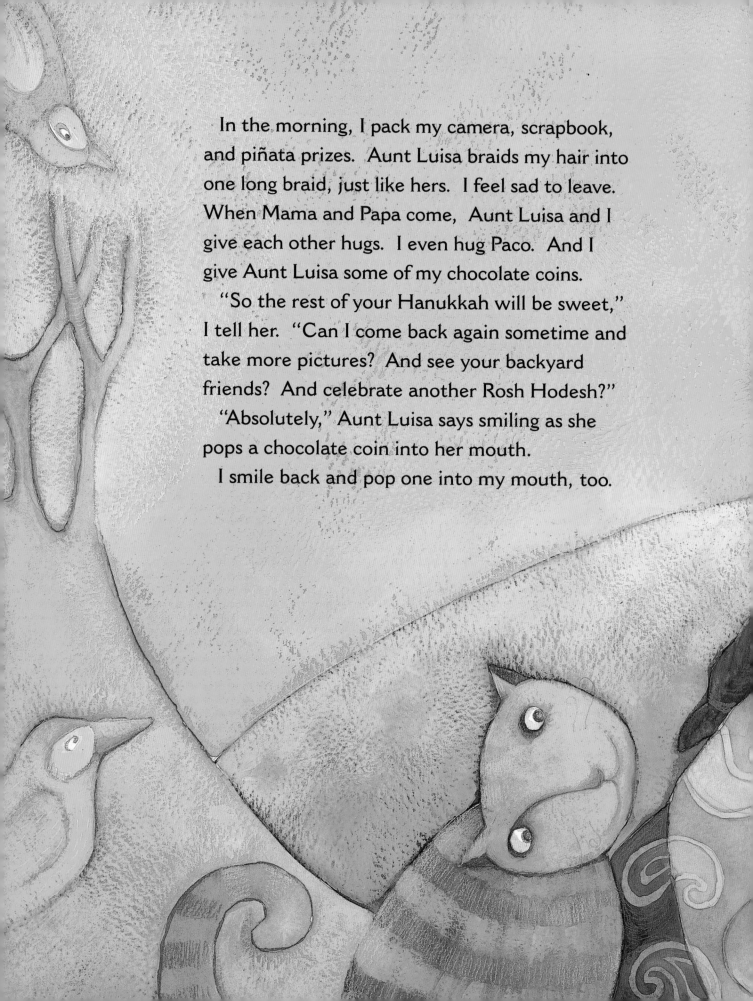

In the morning, I pack my camera, scrapbook, and piñata prizes. Aunt Luisa braids my hair into one long braid, just like hers. I feel sad to leave. When Mama and Papa come, Aunt Luisa and I give each other hugs. I even hug Paco. And I give Aunt Luisa some of my chocolate coins.

"So the rest of your Hanukkah will be sweet," I tell her. "Can I come back again sometime and take more pictures? And see your backyard friends? And celebrate another Rosh Hodesh?"

"Absolutely," Aunt Luisa says smiling as she pops a chocolate coin into her mouth.

I smile back and pop one into my mouth, too.

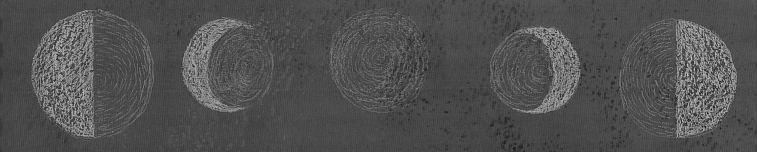

GLOSSARY

COUSCOUS: A Middle-Eastern dish of crushed bulgar wheat combined with meat, vegetables, or fruit.

DREIDEL: A four-sided spinning top used to play games on Hanukkah.

HANUKKAH: The eight-day Festival of Lights which commemorates the victory of the Maccabees, a small band of Jewish patriots, against the mighty Syrian Army, and the rededication of the Temple in Jerusalem. The word Hanukkah means "dedication."

LATKES: Fried potato pancakes—a traditional Hanukkah food.

MENORAH/HANUKKIAH: The menorah was the seven-branch candelabra used in the ancient Temple in Jerusalem. The menorah used to celebrate Hanukkah is also called a hanukkiah. It has nine branches, one for each night and an extra to hold the helper candle used to light the others.

PIÑATA: A colorful container filled with candy and toys, popular at Mexican celebrations.

ROSH HODESH: The first day of the month when the new moon appears. The Rosh Hodesh that falls during Hanukkah ushers in the new month of Tevet.

YARMULKE: A skullcap, called a kipah in Hebrew.

SPANISH PRONUNCIATION GUIDE:

FELIZ JANUCA: (fuh-LEEZ HAH-noo-kah)

LO HICE DE BARRO: (loh EE-say deh BAH-roh)

LUNA NUEVA: (LOO-na noo-EH-vah)

TROMPO: (TROM-poh)

Kar Ben Publishing
A division of Lerner Publishing Group, Inc.
241 First Avenue North
Minneapolis, MN 55401 U.S.A.

Website address: www.karben.com

Library of Congress Cataloging-in-Publication Data
da Costa, Deborah.
Hanukkah moon / by Deborah da Costa ; illustrated by Gosia Mosz.
p. cm.
Summary: When Isobel visits her Aunt Luisa at Hanukkah, she not only has a wonderful time, she learns some new things about this special holiday.
ISBN-13: 978-1-58013-244-2 (lib. bdg. : alk. paper)
ISBN-10: 1-58013-244-8 (lib. bdg. : alk. paper)
1. Hanukkah--Juvenile fiction. 2. Rosh Hodesh--Juvenile fiction.
[1. Hanukkah--Fiction. 2. Rosh Hodesh--Fiction. 3. Aunts--Fiction.
4. Judaism--Customs and practices--Fiction. 5. Photography--Fiction.]
I. Mosz, Gosia, ill. II. Title.
PZ7.D122Han 2007
[E]--dc22   2006027430

Manufactured in the United States of America
3 4 5 6 7 8 – DP – 13 12 11 10 09 08